FATHER CHRISTMAS'S LAST PRESENT

FATHER
CHRISTMAS'S
LAST
PRESENT

Marie-Aude Murail
and Elvire Murail

illustrated by
Quentin Blake

JONATHAN CAPE • LONDON

Since his parents couldn't stop talking about Father Christmas, Julien had decided to pretend to believe in him for another year. So he had written him a letter to ask for a present.

"But a proper big present, Mum," he had insisted. He wanted a video-game console, like his cousin Patrick. His mother thought it would be too expensive.

"Father Christmas can afford that sort of thing," Julien reassured her.

On Christmas morning, Julien ran to the sitting-room. His mother was there, ready for her "Oh-ing" and "Ah-ing". His father appeared, looking sleepy and carrying his cup of coffee in his hand. Julien could see straight away that Father Christmas *had* been able to afford that sort of thing . . .

"Is it what you wanted?" asked his mother.

"The same as Patrick's," said Julien approvingly.

"Make the most of it," said his father. "When you're a big boy Father Christmas will stop coming . . . "

"Oh! Look!" cried Julien's mother. "There's another parcel under the Christmas tree!" She leant down and picked up a box wrapped in some dull brown paper.

"Ah! What can it be?"

This time her "Oh's" and "Ah's" sounded genuine. She really was surprised. So was his father.

Julien tore off the paper. There, in a rather odd-looking cardboard box, was a little wooden steam train. It was painted red and blue and looked really lovely.

"It's a little kid's toy," muttered his father, looking at his wife.

"It wasn't me!" she protested.

"It's got eyes!" cried Julien.

He shouted so loud that he made his parents jump.

"Er . . . yes. It's got eyes," said his father.

"It's looking at me!" Julien wasn't completely certain, but it did seem as though it had winked with one of its eyes. The left one.

"You know this train isn't yours, don't you?" said his father. "It must have fallen out of Father Christmas's sack . . . it's only if nobody claims it within a year and a day that it's yours."

He explained that that was the rule: if you find something, and nobody comes to claim it, at the end of a year and a day you can keep it.

Julien took the little train to his room. He had decided she was called Juliette.

All through the day Julien played with Juliette. He made her a track out of his comic books to run on. (She didn't roll very well on the carpet.)

In the evening Julien put Juliette on a shelf opposite his bed. As it got dark Juliette's eyes started to shine.

The next day cousin Patrick came to the house to play. He soon found himself all alone in front of the video game.

"Why isn't Julien playing with you?" asked his mother.

"Because I wanted to have a crash with his train and he didn't like it."

That day Juliette sat up at the
dinner table with Julien and that
night she rested on his pillow.

"My Julien – he's still just a little
boy," said his mother tenderly.

But his father wasn't happy.
He said to Julien: "It's hardly worth
buying— It's hardly worth Father
Christmas bringing you a video
console as expensive as that if
you're not going to play with it!"

January was just like December except that one thing in life had changed. On a shelf in his bedroom, Juliette waited for Julien to come home from school.

The months passed. Juliette went on holiday. She didn't like the beach because the sand got into her funnel.

What she preferred was the
countryside and nice smooth paths.

On his birthday that year Julien
reached the age when Father
Christmas doesn't visit you
any more.

Christmas Eve arrived. Julien was standing on a chair hanging the decorations on the tree.

"Have you done your letter to Father Christmas?" his mother asked.

"But I'm too old now, Mummy," said Julien.

"You're still allowed to write to him," said his mother, "just one last time."

Julien nearly fell off his chair. Of course! It was time for Father Christmas again!

"A year and a day," his father had said. Father Christmas was a creature of habit – Christmas Eve was when he did all his work. And from one Christmas Eve to another was only a year. Father Christmas was going to come and take back his steam train.

Julien got down from his chair and started thinking. What could he do to keep hold of Juliette?

"Mum, when you've been naughty, Father Christmas doesn't come, does he?" he asked, with a faint glimmer of hope.

"In your case, my darling, there's absolutely nothing to worry about," said his mother, giving him a kiss.

Why, oh why, had he given back the Mickey Mouse eraser he had pinched from Jeremy? He ought to have tipped over the dustbins in the stairwell to annoy that grumpy old cleaning-lady.

He ought to have made fun of his granddad when he muddled up dates and forgot things.

He ought to have— but it was too late now to turn into a monster. "Mum, can't we put off Christmas Eve this year? We could do it tomorrow, couldn't we?"

"Don't be so silly. Go and do your letter."

Julien went to his room,
looked at Juliette and took
up his pen.

"Dear Father Christmas,

With all the children there are everywhere, you really must have an awful lot of work. I am a big boy now, so it really isn't worth the trouble of tiring yourself out for me. My parents can do the shopping for you."

His mother wanted to read the letter before he posted it. She burst out laughing, and then whispered in Julien's ear: "He'll come, my sweet, don't you worry."

Things were really desperate. Julien opened the number 24 on his Advent Calendar and ate the chocolate that was behind the little window. The days had gone past with frightening speed. Christmas Eve already!

That night Julien went to bed early. He had tried everything, thought of everything – even running off with Juliette to a foreign country. There was only one thing left for him to do. But it needed a lot of courage.

After his parents had gone to bed, Julien got up and wrote a last letter to Father Christmas:

"Dear Father Christmas,

You lost this steam train exactly a year ago. I have taken good care of her. The paint is a bit damaged underneath, but it wasn't my fault. It was my cousin Patrick, he derailed her. With a touch of red paint she will be as good as new."

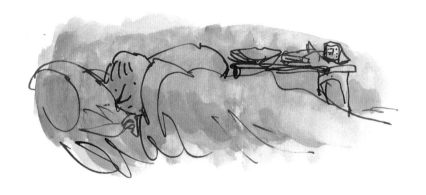

Then Julien remembered that
Father Christmas would not be
visiting him again after this and he
concluded, "Goodbye! Julien."

He tiptoed down to the sitting-room. The garlands of electric lights winked in the shadows. Julien crouched down by the tree.
In one hand he held his letter and with the other he clasped Juliette.
A tear fell on the carpet. If it wasn't Julien who was crying, it could only have been Juliette.

In the morning Julien jumped out of bed. He ran to the sitting-room because, after all, it was Christmas. He pushed open the door and saw straight away that his letter had gone. His parents appeared behind him, cups of coffee in hand.

What was the point of rushing on Christmas morning when you were a grown-up?

Julien turned to them and said simply, "He's been."

Behind Juliette, lined up one after the other, were four little trucks in all the colours of the rainbow: Father Christmas's last present.

FATHER CHRISTMAS'S LAST PRESENT
A JONATHAN CAPE BOOK 978 0224 07021 8
(from January 2007)
0 224 07021 5

Published in Great Britain by Jonathan Cape,
an imprint of Random House Children's Books

First published in *Astrapi* magazine, Bayard Presse, in 1992
This edition published 2003

3 5 7 9 10 8 6 4 2

RANDOM HOUSE CHILDREN'S BOOKS
61-63 Uxbridge Road, London W5 5SA
A division of The Random House Group Ltd

RANDOM HOUSE AUSTRALIA (PTY) LTD
20 Alfred Street, Milsons Point, Sydney,
New South Wales 2061, Australia

RANDOM HOUSE NEW ZEALAND LTD
18 Poland Road, Glenfield, Auckland 10, New Zealand

RANDOM HOUSE (PTY) LTD
Isle of Houghton, Corner Boundary Road & Carse O'Gowrie, Houghton 2198, South Africa

THE RANDOM HOUSE GROUP Limited Reg. No. 954009
www.**kids**a**trandomhouse**.co.uk
www.**kids**a**trandomhouse**.co.uk/quentinblake

A CIP catalogue record for this book is available from the British Library.

Printed and bound in Singapore